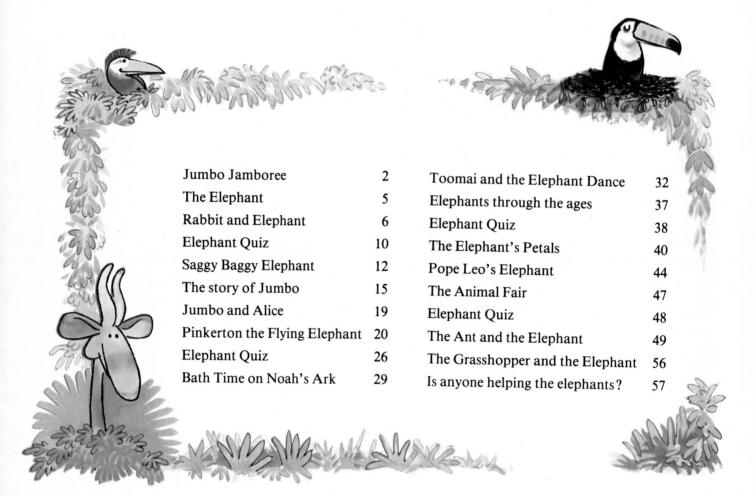

Acknowledgments

Cover and title page illustrations are by James Hodgson, and the endpapers are by Jane Purkiss. Keith Logan illustrated the jokes, and the poems on pages 19, 47, and 56. The bottom drawing on page 37 is by B H Robinson, taken from the Ladybird *Dinosaurs* book, and the line drawing on that page is by Keith Logan.

Factual material for the elephant quizzes was supplied by Robert Howard BA.

Permission to include copyright material has been granted as follows: by George Allen and Unwin, for 'The Elephant's Petals' from *The Elephant and the Flower* by Brian Patten; by BBC Hulton Picture Library for the photographs on pages 18 and 19; by the Trustees of the British Museum for 'Springcleaning on Noah's Ark' by Heath Robinson on page 28; by Jonathan Cape Ltd and the Estates of Geoffrey Boumphey and Kenneth Walker for 'Bathtime on Noah's Ark' from *The Log of the Ark* by Geoffrey Boumphey and Kenneth Walker; by Andre Deutsch Ltd and Houghton Mifflin Company for 'The Ant and the Elephant' by Bill Peet; by Faber and Faber Ltd for 'Jumbo Jamboree' from *Another Six and Twenty Tales* by Peggy Stack; by Tim Graham for the photographs on page 38; by Hamish Hamilton Ltd for 'Pope Leo's Elephant' from *Pope Leo's Elephant* by John Lawrence and 'The story of Jumbo' from *Jumbo the Elephant* by Eric Mathieson; by William Heinemann Ltd and Macmillan Publishing Co Inc for 'The Elephant' by Herbert Asquith; by Hodder and Stoughton Children's Books for 'Rabbit and Elephant' from *Folk Tales* by Leila Berg; by the National Trust and Macmillan, London, Ltd for 'Toomai and the Elephant Dance' from *The Jungle Book* by Rudyard Kipling; by The Natural History Photographic Agency for the photographs on pages 10, 11, 26, 27, 39, 48 and 57; by Ward Lock Ltd for 'Pinkerton the Flying Elephant' by William D'Enno; and by Western Publishing Co Inc for 'Saggy Baggy Elephant' by K and B Jackson, copyright 1947 by Western Publishing Co Inc.

First Edition

The Ladybird
ELEPHANT
BOOK

compiled by
KATIE WALES

The Jumbo Jamboree

by Peggy Stack

illustrated by Bryan Shepard

In the clearing of the jungle, the Jumbo Jamboree for the younger elephants was nearly over and only the obstacle-race remained.

Junior, the smallest elephant, hadn't won a thing.

'You just don't try,' said his Ma. 'You could easy have won the Young Tuskers' race with all that start you were allowed, only you were so slow getting going, like always.'

'My legs seem to have to think before I can get trotting,' said Junior apologetically.

'Shucks,' said his mother. 'Now you just go in and win that obstacle-race, or your Pa and me won't be able to hold up our heads for shame.'

Junior blew a snuffly sigh down his diminutive trunk. It was terrible to be so *backward*.

2

None of the other elephants of his age had to tell their legs what to do before they trotted. They were tall and lanky; he was small and round-about. And worst of all, every Young Tusker had a fine pair of jutting tusks, while his own were no more than two little white knobs that hadn't begun to protrude an inch beyond his cheeks.

But his self-pity was cut short by a sharp push from his mother on his little round behind.

'Get on. They're lining up for the start.'

'I'll never win against all those big fellers,' said Junior hopelessly.

'You can try,' said his Ma.

Junior knew all about the obstacle-race course and hadn't liked what he had seen of it. There was the length of the wide clearing down which you had to run, first of all; at the end of the clearing, a pile of logs waiting to be picked up and carried a hundred yards; then the river to cross; then a felled tree to balance along; and lastly a great big net pegged to the ground that you had to squirm under. It all looked dreadful, and there was miles and miles of it.

Junior trudged along to the starting line and heard one of the growing tuskers snort: 'Here comes the Tuskless Wonder!' and there was a general rumbling guffaw as he was roughly shoved into position.

Then the elephant who was doing the umpiring said: 'You all know the rules. Then, ready, steady, *go!*'

Junior got knocked down almost at once. There didn't seem to *be* any rules, not against bumping and boring, at any rate. Doggedly he scrambled to his feet and urged himself forward again.

'*Oom*petty, puffety, *oom*petty, puffety,' muttered Junior – which was his own private way of encouraging his four, short, reluctant legs into a canter.

At the pile of logs he stopped to get his breath. Now what was it his mother had told him? – *Always get a log well balanced in the middle before you try to lift it.* Curling his trunk cleverly round one of the logs, Junior was pleased to find himself overtaking several of the elephants who were being a bit careless.

'He's doing that prettily,' said one of the watching spectators.

'Ah, but he's gone and dropped it, the silly young shaver!' said another.

Cussing in a way that would have scandalised his mother, Junior went back for another log. (*Beastly* obstacle-races!) This time he got on better and finished the hundred yards, but the other competitors were a long way in front of him.

(*Oom*petty, puffety – have to catch up with them somehow. He'd got to *try*.)

The river lay ahead.

Junior had never crossed the river without holding on to his mother's tail. What were you supposed to *do*, to get safely over all by yourself? The bigger elephants seemed to be making heavy weather of it and quite a lot of them were sinking knee-deep into the mud. 'Oh, well, I dare say I'll drown,' said Junior hopelessly, and did a sprawling belly-flop into the water.

He heard it roaring about his ears, and as he came to the surface, spluttering, caught a bellow from the further bank: 'Keep your *trunk* up, you little chump!' Well, if it wasn't his Pa come along to keep an eye on things! – That made everything *much* better!

3

Raising his small trunk like a periscope and never taking his eyes off his father, he found himself swimming clear of the mud and reached the other side.

'Get on, get on,' said Junior's Pa.

'Where to?' said Junior, who was bemused after his struggles.

'Over to the felled tree, you small juggins! You'll catch up with the others yet.'

(*Oom*petty, puffety.)

While he teetered along the felled tree he nearly gave up hope, for every one of the elephants was ahead of him. Why wasn't his Ma there to encourage him? – It was *her* turn.

And then he heard her shrill, excited voice among the spectators and could hardly believe his ears, because what she trumpeted, quite distinctly, was: 'Keep going, little son, keep going! You're going to *win*!'

Win? His poor old Mum must be barmy.

Then he reached the net and understood.

At first he couldn't make out what was going on among the plunging, snorting, heaving bodies jostling each other under the net. But then one thing became joyfully and gloriously clear – that if you are trying to crawl under a net that is firmly pegged to the ground, *it is a most frightful drawback to have jutting tusks*! The elephants, caught in all directions, were marvellously entangled at that moment.

Junior looked at them. Then he gave a triumphant squeal, and got down on his knees and shoved. (And really, if your tusks are no more than little knobs below your cheeks, crawling under a net is as easy as pie.)

Junior was out on the far side in a moment, and the winning-post lay ahead.

'You see?' said Junior's Ma. 'You had only to try. Your Pa and me knew all along you'd only just to keep going till you reached the net, to win.'

'Where *is* Pa?' said Junior, from where he was lying resting very comfortably beneath his mother's belly.

'Pegging down the net firmer so they can't cheat. They're still there and likely to be so for a long time yet if your Pa has his way. He took mighty offence, your Pa, when they called you the Tuskless Wonder.'

'It's not such a bad name,' said Junior. 'I won, didn't I?'

FINISH

The Elephant
by Herbert Asquith
illustrated by Kathie Layfield

Here comes the elephant
Swaying along
With his cargo of children
All singing a song:
To the tinkle of laughter
He goes on his way,
And his cargo of children
Have crowned him with May.

His legs are in leather
And padded his toes;
He can root up an oak
With a whisk of his nose:
With a wave of his trunk
And a turn of his chin
He can pull down a house,
Or pick up a pin.

Beneath his grey forehead
A little eye peers!
Of what is he thinking
Between those wide ears?
Of what does he think?
If he wishes to tease,
He could twirl his keeper
Over the trees:

If he were not kind,
He could play cup and ball
With Robert and Helen
And Uncle Paul:
But that grey forehead,
Those crinkled ears,
Have learned to be kind
In a hundred years!
And so with the children
He goes on his way
To the tinkle of laughter
And crowned with the May.

Rabbit and Elephant

by Leila Berg
illustrated by
Brian Price Thomas

Rabbit and Elephant were friends. One day they were very hungry. 'We'll have to do some work,' said Rabbit. 'Then we can get some food.'

They went together to a farmer who lived nearby, and Rabbit said, 'Will you give us some beans to eat if we work in your fields?'

'Certainly I will,' said the farmer. 'But you'll have to work properly, you know.'

'Of course we will,' said Rabbit. Elephant said nothing. When the farmer looked at him, he just made a sort of coughing noise.

Now the farmer could see Rabbit and Elephant were really hungry, so he gave them the beans right away, and they put them in the pot to cook while they were working.

So there were the beans cooking away in the pot, and there were Rabbit and Elephant working away in the fields.

Rabbit worked and worked. But Elephant didn't work at all. He kept saying how hot it was, and how hard it was, and that his foot hurt, and that his ear hurt, and that the grass was prickly, and that something was biting him. And he'd keep going away to have a drink, and whenever he came back he'd say, 'Oh look, you've hardly anything left to do. And look how much I have!'

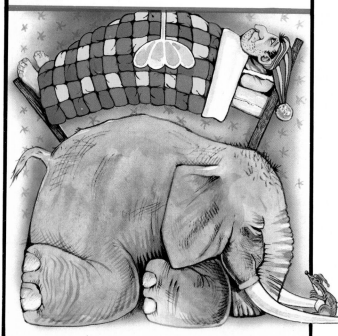

HOW...

How can you tell if there is an elephant under your bed?

When you're nearly touching the ceiling.

6

So Rabbit thought, 'Oh dear, I suppose I'll have to help him, or he'll never get finished.'

And that's how it happened that when Rabbit had finished all her own work, instead of sitting down and eating her beans – for she was very hungry – she started on Elephant's work instead. Even then, Elephant didn't help. He said he had to go off to get some banana leaves to keep his forehead cool, because he had a headache.

Rabbit worked away, hungrier and hotter, till it was all done. Then Elephant came back, and the two of them walked over to their cooking-pot and looked at their beans cooking away there. Oh, they did smell good.

Rabbit was just going to take some at last, when Elephant said, 'Don't take them yet. I just have to have a wash. You won't start without me, will you?' So Rabbit, who was so very hungry after all the work she'd done, looked sadly at the bubbling, steaming beans, and said politely, 'No, of course I won't start without you, Elephant.'

Off went Elephant to the river, and hid in the tall, wavy grass. And there he quickly undid his sixteen buttons – for in those days an Elephant's coat still buttoned down the front with sixteen buttons – and he stepped out of his coat, one leg, two legs, three legs, four legs, folded it tidily and left it on the grass.

Well, Rabbit was sitting by the beans, wishing Elephant would hurry up, when suddenly – 'RRRRRRah!' something frightful rushed at her, something enormous. It was as big as an elephant, but so peculiar looking. Rabbit left the beans, and ran and ran.

It was a little while before she felt brave enough to come back. She came through the grass, stepping very quietly on the tips of her toes. It was all right. The monster had gone. But so had the beans.

Soon Elephant came back from the river. He looked very happy. 'Are the beans ready?' he called.

'Oh, Elephant,' said Rabbit. 'A terrible thing has happened. A monster has come and eaten all the beans.'

'I don't believe it,' said Elephant. 'You've eaten them yourself, you greedy thing.'

'Oh no,' said Rabbit. 'You know I wouldn't.'

'Well, it can't be helped,' said Elephant. 'We'll just have to go to bed without any beans.'

So that was how the first day ended.

Next day the farmer gave them more work and more beans. They put them on to cook the same as before, and Rabbit worked hard, so hard, while Elephant did nothing. He said his toe was blistered, and his tail had got bent, and he had something in his eye.

And at last Elephant went away to wash, and in the long, wavy grass he undid all his sixteen buttons and stepped out of his coat, one leg, two legs, three legs, four legs, folded it tidily and left it on the grass.

And you know what happened next. Rabbit, sitting by the bubbling beans, was chased away by an enormous monster, as big as an elephant, but so peculiar looking. And when she came back, stepping so quietly on the tips of her toes, the monster had gone — and so had the beans.

'I bet you ate them yourself,' said Elephant, when Rabbit told him.

'No, I didn't,' said Rabbit. 'You know I didn't.'

'Well, it can't be helped,' said Elephant. 'We'll have to go to bed without any beans.'

'All right,' said Rabbit. 'But you know what I'm going to do? Before I go to bed, I'm going to look for some wood, and I'm going to make a bow and arrow, and if that monster comes again to take our beans, I'll shoot him dead.'

Later that evening, Elephant said to Rabbit, 'Oh, Rabbit, did you make a bow and arrow?'

'Yes, I did,' said Rabbit.

'You'd better let me have a look at it,' said Elephant. 'I know a lot about bows and arrows, and I can tell you if it's a good one.'

So Rabbit brought her bow and arrow, and Elephant looked at it and said, 'Mmmmmmm. Not bad at all. There's just a little bit here I'll make right for you.' And he got out his knife and cut away for a bit, and at last he said, 'Ah, that's better. That'll be all right now. I'm glad you showed me that.'

Then they went to bed and that was how the second day ended.

Next day, they went to work again, while the beans cooked in the pot. Rabbit worked hard. Elephant made excuses. Then just the same as before, the monster came rushing at Rabbit as she sat by the cooking-pot waiting for Elephant to come back from the river. But this time Rabbit picked up her bow and arrow and shot at him. 'Crack!' The bow broke. Wasn't that just the place where Elephant had been cutting it with his knife?

Well, off ran Rabbit as fast as she could, with the monster after her. When she came back, all the beans were gone.

'Did you catch the monster?' called Elephant.

'No. The bow broke.'

'Really! I am surprised!' And Elephant hid his smile with his curly trunk.

Rabbit didn't notice Elephant smiling, but she had suddenly begun to wonder what an Elephant would look like if he undid all the sixteen buttons of his coat and stepped right out of it, one leg, two legs, three legs, four legs. She wondered about this all evening, for by now she was very hungry indeed. The next morning she got up early and made herself a new bow and arrow and hid them in the grass.

Everything happened the same as before. Rabbit worked hard. Elephant did nothing. He was tired, he felt sick, he was thirsty. Off he went to the river at last, to have his wash. And in a minute or two, on came the roaring monster.

But this time as soon as Rabbit saw the roaring monster, she picked up her new bow and arrow from the grass, and aimed very carefully.

'Ow!' shouted the Elephant. 'You horrid thing! You've hurt me! What did you do that for? Fancy being so mean, just for a few beans! I'll probably die!'

But Rabbit was very angry. 'A fine friend you are!' she said. 'You won't die. It's only a prick. Now go and wash yourself properly this time, and put on your coat, and don't you dare play any tricks on me again.'

So Elephant went slowly back to the river, and really did wash himself this time, and put on his coat, and did up all the sixteen buttons, and behaved properly. And Rabbit sat down by the bubbling, steaming beans, and, at last, ate them all up.

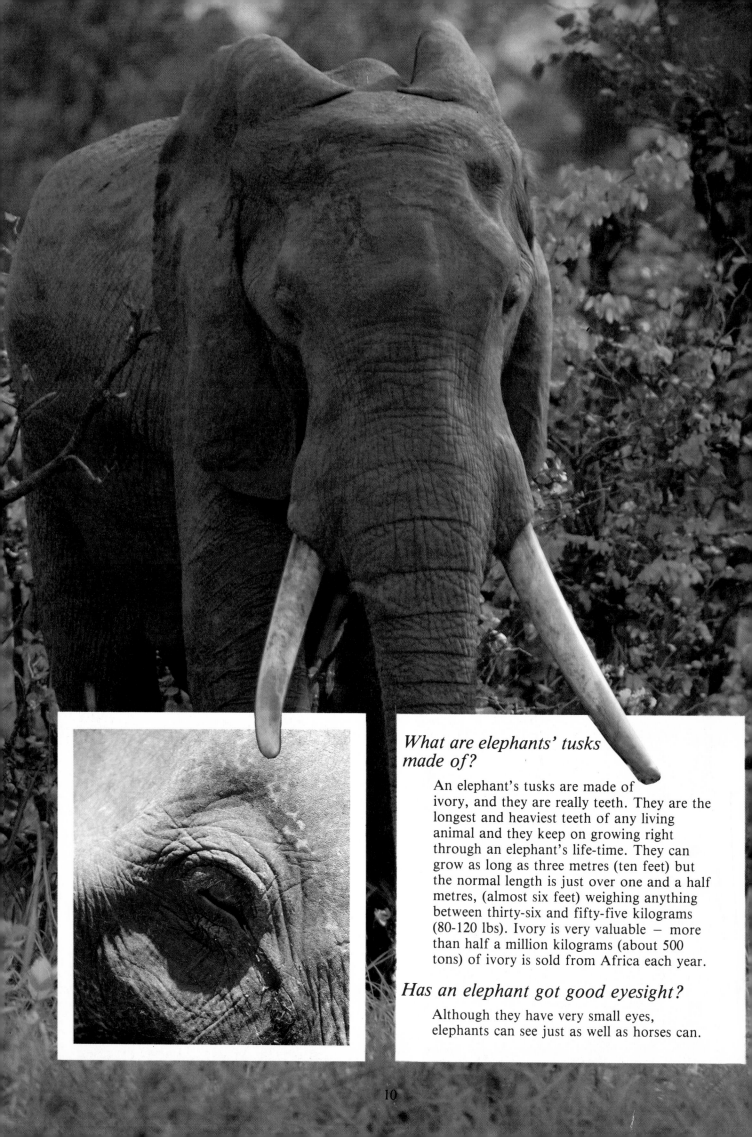

What are elephants' tusks made of?

An elephant's tusks are made of ivory, and they are really teeth. They are the longest and heaviest teeth of any living animal and they keep on growing right through an elephant's life-time. They can grow as long as three metres (ten feet) but the normal length is just over one and a half metres, (almost six feet) weighing anything between thirty-six and fifty-five kilograms (80-120 lbs). Ivory is very valuable — more than half a million kilograms (about 500 tons) of ivory is sold from Africa each year.

Has an elephant got good eyesight?

Although they have very small eyes, elephants can see just as well as horses can.

Is an elephant's skin thick?

Although the elephant's skin *(hide)* is between two and four centimetres (¾-1½ inches) thick, it is very sensitive. Elephants look after their skin very carefully — they wash and massage it, and even powder it!

Do elephants remember everything?

They don't really have perfect memories, but they do seem to remember people who have been kind to them (or cruel to them) for as long as twenty years, in zoos and circuses. In the wild, they must have a good memory to remember all the others in the herd — there may be as many as fifty!

Why do elephants have trunks?

An elephant's head is so heavy that it needs a short, strong neck to support it. This means that it cannot reach its food on the ground, so elephants need trunks to pick up food and place it in their mouths.

The elephant also breathes and smells through its trunk, using it as a nose — elephants have a very good sense of smell.

What do elephants eat?

They only eat things like grasses, leaves, roots and shoots because they are *herbivorous,* which means that they do not eat meat (animals which eat meat are *carnivorous*). Because of their great size, elephants need enormous amounts of food each day. A wild African elephant needs between 250 and 350 kilograms (550-750 lbs) of food each day, and can spend up to twenty hours of the day simply eating. In zoos, elephants eat a great deal of hay, as well as titbits of oats, beets and potatoes.

11   *Elephant facts researched by Robert Howard* BA

Saggy, Baggy, Elephant

by K and B Jackson
illustrated by Petula Stone

A happy little elephant was dancing through the jungle. He thought he was dancing beautifully, one-two-three-kick. But whenever he went one-two-three, his big feet pounded so that they shook the whole jungle. And whenever he went kick, he kicked over a tree or a bush.

The little elephant danced along leaving wreckage behind him, until one day, he met a parrot.

'Why are you shaking the jungle all to pieces?' cried the parrot, who had never before seen an elephant. 'What kind of animal are you, anyway?'

The little elephant said, 'I don't know what kind of animal I am. I live all alone in the jungle. I dance and I kick – and I call myself Sooki. It's a good-sounding name, and it fits me, don't you think?'

'Maybe,' answered the parrot, 'but if it does it's the only thing that *does* fit you. Your ears are too big for you, and your nose is away too big for you. And your skin is *much*, MUCH too big for you. It's baggy and saggy. You should call yourself Saggy-Baggy!'

Sooki sighed. His pants *did* look pretty wrinkled.

'I'd be glad to improve myself,' he said, 'but I don't know how to go about it. What shall I do?'

'I can't tell you. I never saw anything like you in all my life!' replied the parrot.

The little elephant tried to smooth out his skin. He rubbed it with his trunk. That did no good.

He pulled up his pants' legs – but they fell right back into dozens of wrinkles.

It was very disappointing, and the parrot's saucy laugh didn't help a bit.

Just then a tiger came walking along. He was a beautiful, sleek tiger. His skin fitted him like a glove.

Sooki rushed up to him and said:

'Tiger, please tell me why your skin fits so well! The parrot says mine is all baggy and saggy, and I do want to make it fit me like yours fits you!'

The tiger didn't care a fig about Sooki's troubles, but he did feel flattered and important, and he did feel just a little mite hungry.

'My skin always did fit,' said the tiger. 'Maybe it's because I take a lot of exercise. But . . .' added the tiger, '. . . if you don't care for exercise, I shall be delighted to nibble a few of those extra pounds of skin off for you!'

'Oh no, thank you! No, thank you!' cried Sooki. 'I love exercise! Just watch me!'

Sooki ran until he was well beyond reach.

Then he did somersaults and rolled on his back. He walked on his hind legs and he walked on his front legs.

When Sooki wandered down to the river to get a big drink of water, he met the parrot. The parrot laughed harder than ever.

'I tried exercising,' sighed the little elephant. 'Now I don't know what to do.'

'Soak in the water the way the crocodile does,' laughed the parrot. 'Maybe your skin will shrink.'

So Sooki tramped straight into the water.

But before he had soaked nearly long enough to shrink his skin, a great big

crocodile came swimming up, snapping his fierce jaws and looking greedily at Sooki's tender ears.

The little elephant clambered up the bank and ran away, feeling very discouraged.

'I'd better hide in a dark place where my bags and sags and creases and wrinkles won't show,' he said.

By and by he found a deep dark cave, and with a heavy sigh he tramped inside and sat down.

HOW...

How do you get four elephants into a Mini?

Two in the front, and two in the back.

13

Suddenly, he heard a fierce growling and grumbling and snarling. He peeped out of the cave and saw a lion padding down the path.

'I'm hungry!' roared the lion. 'I haven't had a thing to eat today. Not a thing except a thin, bony antelope, and a puny monkey – and a buffalo, but such a tough one! And two turtles, but you can't count turtles. There's nothing much to eat between those saucers they wear for clothes! I'm *hungry!* I could eat an *elephant!*'

And he began to pad straight towards the dark cave where the little elephant was hidden.

'This is the end of me, sags, bags, wrinkles and all,' thought Sooki, and he let out one last, trumpeting bellow!

Just as he did, the jungle was filled with a terrible crashing and an awful stomping. A whole herd of great, grey wrinkled elephants came charging up, and the big hungry lion jumped up in the air, turned around, and ran away as fast as he could go.

Sooki peeped out of the cave and all the big elephants smiled at him. Sooki thought they were the most beautiful creatures he had ever seen.

'I wish I looked just like you,' he said.

'You do,' grinned the big elephants. 'You're a perfectly dandy little elephant!'

And that made Sooki so happy that he began to dance one-two-three-kick through the jungle, with all those big, brave, friendly elephants behind him. The saucy parrot watched them dance. But this time he didn't laugh, not even to himself.

The story of Jumbo

by Eric Mathieson
illustrated by Drury Lane Studios

When a baby elephant arrived at London Zoo one summer day in 1865, one of the first things that had to be done was to decide upon a name for the new arrival. No one knows quite how the decision was made but, in the end, he was called Jumbo. Today, when you say 'Jumbo,' everyone thinks of an elephant; but then, a hundred years ago, no elephant had ever been given this name.

It was this small, frightened new addition to London Zoo, standing miserably in one corner of the elephant house, who was to make the name famous all over the world . . .

Sometimes Jumbo was mischievous and played games. He would reach down with his trunk and pull off his keeper's cap. Keeper Scott would pretend to be angry while all the watching crowd laughed. Then Jumbo would place the cap gently back again on the man's head. Sometimes, in the afternoon, Jumbo would try to steal some of his keeper's tea. He had his own favourite taste in buns and keeper Scott sometimes found, as well, that Jumbo had emptied his tea cup while he wasn't watching.

It was in a way like this that his keeper discovered Jumbo's strange taste for whisky. It was New Year's Eve and keeper Scott had gone round to the elephant house to wish Jumbo a Happy New Year. He carried a glass in his hand to drink the health of the New Year. Jumbo stretched out an inquisitive trunk and, before Scott realised what was happening, his New Year's drink of whisky had disappeared. Jumbo trumpeted with pleasure.

By this time, Jumbo had grown very large indeed. He was twelve feet high up to his shoulders and he weighed six and a half tons. His trunk was seven feet long and he could reach up to things that were twenty-six feet off the ground. He was quite the biggest elephant that the zoo had ever seen. Every day, he ate 200 pounds of hay, and fifteen loaves of bread, as well as all the sweets and fruit that visitors gave him. He drank five pails of water every day. And, when his strange taste was discovered, he was also allowed a quart of whisky.

The crowds especially liked to see him enjoying his daily ration of this and he became famous as the elephant that liked whisky.

Jumbo was now one of the star attractions at the London Zoo. Many people came every day especially to see him. The enclosure where Jumbo spent most of his mornings and afternoons was always surrounded by visitors. And, every week, hundreds of children and grown-ups were given rides on Jumbo's back.

One day, there was great excitement in the zoo. If Jumbo had not been too busy finishing off a delicious cabbage that he had been given as part of his dinner, he might have seen a large group of people walking towards the elephant enclosure. In the centre of the group was a small, rather plump lady, dressed in black. She was accompanied by several children who seemed very excited. Important-looking zoo officials were explaining things to her.

'And this is the famous Jumbo.'

The small lady nodded her head, gravely. The official went on to explain just how much Jumbo ate (he left out the whisky) and how big and strong he was. The small lady listened very politely. The children were getting more and more excited. One of them tugged at her hand.

'Oh, mamma, can we ride on him, can we have a ride?'

Jumbo looked up at the group of visitors and stretched out his trunk towards them, hoping for something to eat. One of the little girls gave a small scream.

'Just *look* at his long, long trunk!'

'He is hoping to be fed, ma'am,' explained one of the zoo officials. 'It is quite safe.'

'I see,' said the small lady and, accepting something from a paper bag, Queen Victoria gave Jumbo a bun.

Jumbo, in fact, became a great favourite with the Royal Family. The Queen herself visited him several times. He was also visited by the American President, Theodore Roosevelt, who was in London. Many of the royal children and grandchildren were given rides on Jumbo's back. But these were not the only famous passengers he was to carry. One day, among the excited children, crowded on to the high-riding seat, was a small boy with bright red hair. He was holding on very tight, his chin stuck out in a determined way.

'I do hope he won't be frightened,' an anxious lady was saying on the ground beneath.

But the small boy hung on all the tighter, determined not to be frightened. His name was Winston Churchill.

By 1881 Jumbo had lived at the London Zoo for nearly seventeen years. All this time, he had been looked after by his faithful keeper, Matthew Scott.

Towards the end of this time Jumbo had been seen by yet another famous visitor, although no one guessed just how important this visit would turn out to be.

Mr Phineas Taylor Barnum, the famous American circus owner, had seen Jumbo on one of his visits to London. He had even had a ride upon the elephant's back. In 1881 he told his agent to ask the superintendent of the zoo if there was any possibility of buying Jumbo for the circus. Barnum knew what a great success the splendid elephant would be in the circus ring.

At first, the offer was indignantly refused. But later, to everyone's astonishment, the zoo agreed to sell Jumbo to Barnum for the very large sum of £2,000.

Even Barnum himself was surprised by the decision. Later, it was said that Jumbo had recently been having bouts of bad temper and was dangerous. Keeper Scott was most indignant about this and declared that Jumbo was as sweet-natured as a kitten. Perhaps the zoo authorities were just thinking of all the other animals that they could buy with this large sum of money.

No one really knows. What is certain, however, is that the news that Jumbo had been sold to America produced an outburst of anger and indignation.

WHY...

Why do elephants ride bicycles?

Because they're too big for tricycles.

17

Almost overnight, people all over the country discovered that Jumbo was an important part of the British way of life. People who had not been within a hundred miles of London Zoo grew red in the face and angry at the thought of the elephant's being sold. Hundreds of people wrote letters to the newspapers. It was suggested that the agreement with Barnum to sell Jumbo should be broken, no matter how much money this might cost. Queen Victoria and the Prince of Wales both thought that this would be the best thing to do. Questions were asked in Parliament and several of the zoo officials went to law to try to prevent the sale from taking place.

And the whole country went Jumbo mad. Almost every magazine or newspaper contained stories or poems about the famous elephant. The illustrated papers were full of his pictures. You could buy Jumbo hats and Jumbo collars and neckties. You could even smoke special Jumbo cigars. The ladies, when they went to dances, used their special Jumbo fans and danced to the tune of the Jumbo polka. There were lots of popular songs about him.

Someone discovered that there was a female elephant at the zoo called Alice. As a matter of fact, Alice and Jumbo had never got on especially well together. This did not matter. 'Alice will be heartbroken if Jumbo goes,' people said.

The editor of the *Daily Telegraph* cabled to Barnum in America and begged him not to take Jumbo away from London.

'Editor's compliments; all British children distressed at elephant's departure; hundreds of correspondents beg us to inquire on what terms you will kindly return Jumbo.'

Barnum replied that 51,000,000 Americans were anxiously awaiting Jumbo's arrival. He said that his largest circus tent seated 20,000 people and was filled twice each day, and he was determined to have Jumbo.

He wished long life and prosperity to the British Nation, the *Telegraph* and to Jumbo . . .

So Jumbo did go to America after all. He toured with Barnum, and eventually died in 1885.

Jumbo and Alice

Jumbo said to Alice:
'I love you.'
Alice said to Jumbo:
'I don't believe you do;
For if you really loved me,
As you say you do,
You'd never go to Yankee Town
And leave me in the zoo.'

Pinkerton the Flying Elephant

by William D'Enno
illustrated by Brian Price Thomas

Far away in the land of Africa, there are thick, tangled forests, through which it is very hard to pass, since so many branches and grasses block your way. These forests are known as jungles.

Now, in an African jungle there once lived a family of elephants: Father Elephant, Mother Elephant, and their Baby Elephant. He wasn't really known as Baby Elephant at all, though. Everyone called him Pinkerton, and here's why:

When he was very small and too young to wash himself, Mother Elephant would wash him. Elephants are very lucky when it comes to washing: all they have to do is suck lots of water up their trunks, and then squirt it all over themselves.

Well, one day Mother Elephant was in a hurry, and didn't notice that the water from the pool was pink in colour, because all the earth around it was light red, and she sprayed Baby Elephant as usual.

What a shock she got when he turned pink all over! 'Oh, dear! What have I done!' she thought, as she stared at Baby Elephant. He was surely the funniest-looking Elephant in the world!

You can imagine what a surprise all his jungle friends got when they saw him again. At first, they just couldn't believe their eyes.

'Let's call him Pinkerton, shall we?' said Archie the Antelope.

'That's a grand idea!' they all shouted, and from that day on, Pinkerton was Baby Elephant's name.

After a while, Pinkerton grew used to being pink, and even went along to what he called the Pink Pool by himself, so that he could wash in the coloured water, though his mother always told him not to.

One day, when he was busy washing, a huge crocodile was staring at him from behind a clump of reeds.

'Yum, Yum!' it said to itself. 'I wonder whether pink elephants taste better than grey ones?' And off it swam to find out.

Before Pinkerton knew what was happening, he saw the croc only a few yards away and swimming fast. He tried to get away, but just could not reach the shore in time. Then, just as he was about to be swallowed up by the long teethy jaws, a strange thing happened. Pinkerton wildly spun his trunk round and round, and he took off! Yes, he flew straight up into the air, leaving the hungry croc in the pool with his mouth still wide open!

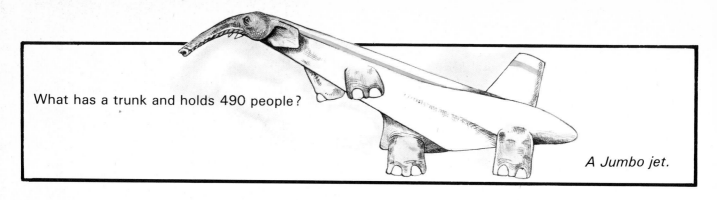

What has a trunk and holds 490 people?

A Jumbo jet.

Pinkerton was jolly glad to get back to his family and the other friendly animals that lived near him. But not one of them believed his story about flying away from a crocodile. Would you?

'All right,' said Pinkerton. 'I'll show you I can fly if you like, shall I?'

All the jungle animals sat around to watch as Pinkerton turned his trunk round and round. He even flapped his ears and tail, but – nothing happened!

How the animals laughed! You could have heard them for miles around.

Poor Pinkerton was so sad that he hadn't been able to fly, and he felt upset for ages afterwards.

One day, a couple of weeks later, he was walking through the jungle all by himself. Usually he went with friends, but now he felt he had no friends left, especially since everyone called him, 'Pinkerton the Flier!'

Suddenly, he heard a growling noise behind him, and he could see a pair of bright yellow eyes staring at him through the thick tangle of branches.

Pinkerton knew straight away that this was a lion — a lion that was so hungry that it was going to hunt down a pink elephant and eat it!

Pinkerton ran. He ran as fast as he could, but all the time he could hear the leaves rustling behind him, and knew that with every step the lion was getting closer and closer. It would only be a few minutes before the huge, roaring beast could attack him, and poor Pinkerton would never see his family and friends again. The lion was really enjoying himself.

He could have caught up with Pinkerton earlier, but he wanted to watch this strange, pink elephant tire himself out first. What fun!

But just then, he saw the elephant's trunk go spinning round and round, and its tail and ears start to flap. What was happening? Suddenly, he saw this funny animal float upwards towards the top branches of a tall tree. Up and up it went, until it was resting on one of the very highest branches.

The lion was so angry at having lost Pinkerton, that he snarled and growled at the foot of the tree for a long time. But really he was amazed.

'A flying elephant!' he said to himself as he walked off through the jungle. 'Who would ever believe it? Well, if an elephant knows how to fly, it jolly well deserves to escape, that's what I think.'

Pinkerton was in the meantime resting and trying to get his breath back. Soon he felt better, and thought that as it was getting dark he ought to start making his way home again.

But do you think he could get down again? Of course not!

Up till now, Pinkerton had always flown upwards, not downwards!

'Oh, well, I'm too tired to try to fly down tonight,' he said.

'I'll just wait up here till the morning.'

Really he was afraid of going through the jungle at night, and also of trying to fly down to the ground. He was sure he would feel braver in the morning.

And so he slowly fell asleep, dreaming about his bed at home, and having a nice wash in the Pink Pool.

Suddenly, the branches moved and sprang up and down, and Pinkerton woke with a start. But it was only the monkeys who lived in the tree.

Pinkerton wondered why they too didn't go to sleep, and was going to ask them, but he didn't know their language.

Morning soon came and Pinkerton felt well and strong again.

'Now to try that branch!' he said.

But as he went nearer to the end of the branch, it began to bend more and more. Pinkerton was frightened and had started to feel dizzy. And everyone knows that even birds can't fly if they feel dizzy.

Poor old Pinkerton! He was well and truly stuck at the top of the tree, and felt so sad that he started crying.

Meanwhile, Mother and Father Elephant had grown really worried, and even some of the other jungle animals were asking what had become of Pinkerton the Flier.

It so happened that Pinkerton's parents asked some monkeys about their son. Now, monkeys know everything about the jungle and always know what is happening because they pass news on so quickly in their funny, chattery language. The monkeys in the tree with Pinkerton soon heard the distress call of their neighbours, and took pity on the Pink Elephant, who was still sobbing away at the end of the long branch.

By passing messages from tree to tree, the monkeys were able to guide Mother and Father Elephant and all the other animals to the foot of the tree.

'How on earth did you manage to get up there, Pinkerton?' they all shouted.

'I'll tell you when I get down,' shouted back Pinkerton.

But no one could think of a way of getting him down! He was far too heavy for the monkeys to carry, and not one of the animals would be able to climb that tree.

After they had all been standing around for some time, a latecomer arrived. It was Gerry the Giraffe, who was just on his way to see a friend.

'What's all the fuss about?' he asked.

When he had been told the full story, he said:

'Leave this to me. I'll get Pinkerton down in a jiffy!'

All he did was stretch his neck so that the elephant could slide down it to safety. What a funny feeling it was for Pinkerton to slide down Gerry's neck. In a couple of seconds he was back on the ground with his parents and friends.

Pinkerton was the hero of the day. All the animals lifted him up on to their backs, and they all started singing 'For he's a jolly good flier!'

It was only when they got nearer home that a few of the animals asked him how he had come to be on the top branch of a tree.

'I know you won't believe me,' replied Pinkerton, 'but I flew. I was being chased by a lion, and I got so frightened that I just took off!'

Still the animals of the jungle could not believe his story, until one day when Pinkerton was out near the Pink Pool with a few friends. A crocodile saw them coming, but as soon as it saw Pinkerton it turned and fled! It was the same croc who had chased him once before, and he was really afraid of Pinkerton now.

On the way home they saw a lion. As Pinkerton drew nearer – WHOOSH! The lion ran off! Just like that!

From that day on, all the animals of the jungle – big and small – believed the strange story of Pinkerton the Flying Elephant.

Do elephants wash themselves?

Yes – and they even take a shower, because they shower themselves with their trunks. They always bath in very clear pure water because they drink lots of water while bathing – sometimes as much as fourteen bucketfuls!

Elephants don't like to be too hot. During the hottest part of the day, they will stay in the shade of the forest. To keep themselves cool they like to slosh about in mud, and they also fan themselves with their ears.

Do elephants ever go to sleep?

Yes, but they only need to sleep for a short time – between two and four hours a day. They often sleep standing up, although they prefer to lie down, and they wake up from time to time to check for danger.

26

Can elephants swim?

Elephants are very good swimmers – they cross deep rivers as much as two kilometres (one and a quarter miles) wide. When they swim they hold their trunks up like a snorkel to breathe through.

How big is an elephant?

The biggest elephant ever recorded was in Africa in 1955. It weighed over 9,000 kilograms (ten tons) and stood four metres (thirteen feet) high *at the shoulder!*

The elephant is the biggest living land animal – of all the animals on Earth, only whales grow bigger than elephants.

African elephants are the biggest and are usually from three to four metres high, weighing up to 7,500 kilograms (eight and a quarter tons).

How does an elephant drink?

It sucks water into its trunk, and then takes it into its mouth.

SPRING CLEANING IN NOAH'S ARK.

W. HEATH ROBINSON

Bathtime on Noah's Ark

by Geoffrey Boumphey and Kenneth Walker
illustrated by Bobbie Spargo

When the Elephant choked it was quite an event on board, though perhaps not as amusing for the Elephant as for the others.

It happened just before breakfast one morning, when most people had had their baths and had gone back to their cabins. The Giraffe was the first person to discover that something was wrong with his big friend, whom he had found all alone in the bath-room, choking and spluttering, and making noises rather like a bath emptying. Her great sides shook with coughing, and every now and then she gave so tremendous a sneeze that it surely must have been heard all over the Ark.

Altogether it was so alarming, that the Giraffe turned to seek help; but already those in neighbouring cabins were hurrying along to see whatever all the strange noises could be; and they now streamed into the bath-room and all crowded round the Elephant, their mouths open with wonder at the giant heaves and spasms that shook her frame.

'Why, she's choking, poor dear!' cried the Kangaroo. 'Thump her on the back, someone!' But no one was tall enough, and though the Monkey climbed up and hammered away importantly, his little fists had no more effect than a fly walking about, while the next sneeze shot him on to the heads of the others below.

'That's no use,' said the Yak. 'Try something sensible, or she'll burst, for certain. She's swallowed something – that's what she's done, and it's gone the wrong way.'

'Yes, but which *is* her right way?' said the Kangaroo, rather nettled with the Yak.

A puzzled look spread over the Yak's face. 'Well, now I come to think of it – I'm not very sure – for an elephant. We must try and make her speak.'

So all the animals shouted at the Elephant, begging her to tell them what was wrong. She tried very hard in between the sneezes and chokes; and this is what they heard:

'Hunk! – Ksnork! – BY BATH – Atschoo! – Khairk! – STUCK – Gahh! – BY TRONK – Atschoo! – Ssnork!'

This did not seem to help much, and everyone looked very worried. Then the Otter stepped forward. 'I've got it,' he said. 'She's been drinking the bath-water again, and something has got up her trunk and stuck there.'

'Yes, but there's nothing in the bath to get up it,' said the Yak.

'Perhaps it was a little Frog,' suggested the Kangaroo tearfully.

'Nonsense,' snorted the Camel; 'the Frogs are all up on deck, enjoying the rain.'

'I know,' said the Monkey suddenly. 'It's my soap! I left it in the bath by mistake.'

29

Everyone turned
and looked at the Monkey,
who had made his way through
the crowd again, and, having caught
hold of the end of the Elephant's trunk,
was peering up it as if it was a telescope.
Suddenly the Elephant sneezed, and the
Monkey was blown right across the bath-room.
Everyone shouted with laughter as he picked
himself up.

'What do you mean — your soap?' said
the Yak, when he could speak — a Yak does
not often laugh, but when he does he finds it
very difficult to stop. 'You don't use soap.'

'Of course I do,' replied the Monkey
haughtily. 'As a matter of fact, I borrowed
some from Cousin Japhet's cabin, but I lost
it in the bath.'

'Well, the Elephant's found it for you,'
sniggered the Camel. 'You'd better get it
back.'

The Monkey scratched his head. 'Yes,' he
said, after a pause; 'but it's such a long
way up.'

'Tell her to hold her nose and take a drink
of water,' suggested the Kangaroo; 'that's
the way to stop hiccups.'

'She hasn't got hiccups,' snapped the
Camel; 'and what's more, if she holds her
nose she can't drink — so that's no use.'

The Kangaroo looked hurt and said no
more. There really seemed nothing to be
done to help the poor Elephant; and
everyone was feeling very depressed, when
the wise Marabou Stork looked in on his
way to breakfast — for the bell had rung,
although no one had noticed it.

A path was made for him through the
crowd, and he stood by the Elephant,
looking very wise, while the case was
explained to him. He thought for a moment,
with his head on one side, while everyone
watched anxiously; and then he spoke: 'It
should be quite simple. Soap, I think you

said. That will dissolve in water. She must
drink water and squirt it out again until the
soap is dissolved.'

'Just what I said,' put in the Kangaroo.
But no one took any notice of her; they were
too busy guiding the poor Elephant to the
bath, and urging her to put her trunk in and
drink.

There was a moment's silence except for the gurgle of the water as it filled her trunk; then, just as it was nearly full, she sneezed and spoilt it all — as well as drenching everyone around with the spray. However, the second attempt was better and she started to blow it down again. Then suddenly the Last Two Clidders, who had never for an instant taken their eyes off the Elephant, started clapping their hands. 'Oh, look!' they cried. 'She's blowing bubbles. Isn't it clever of her?'

They were quite right, for out of the Elephant's trunk were pouring clouds of enormous bubbles, the biggest and most beautiful bubbles that had ever been blown. They clustered round her trunk and head like huge jewels, gleaming with a thousand wonderful colours as they quivered and shook. Faster and faster they came, more and more every time she emptied her trunk, until the whole room seemed full of them, and the Elephant's form was completely lost in a great cloud of glistening bubbles.

The Kangaroo began to get worried as the cloud got bigger still. 'I suppose she *is* still

in there,' she said hesitatingly. 'I mean . . .' but she got an unexpected answer, as a squirt of soapy water shot out of the mass of bubbles and hit her, filling her pouch to overflowing. 'Dear me!' she said, in a vexed voice, 'and it's always so troublesome to dry inside.'

The bubbles heaved; and out of them came the Elephant, a little hoarse, perhaps, but otherwise none the worse. 'It's gone!' she cried, beaming round; and their faces cleared. Only the Monkey seemed at all worried; he was looking from the Elephant to the shrinking mass of bubbles, and then back at the disappearing form of the Elephant, as she hurried away with the other beasts to breakfast. 'Where's my soap?' he asked anxiously. 'There's something wrong.'

'Yes,' said the Kangaroo. 'They should have held her nose—I said so right from the beginning.'

31

Toomai and the Elephant Dance

by Rudyard Kipling
illustrated by Kathie Layfield

Kala Nag the elephant has served the Indian Government for forty-seven years, and is nearly seventy. His driver is Big Toomai; Little Toomai is his ten year old son. Little Toomai wishes to go elephant-catching, and asks the boss, Petersen Sahib . . .

'Yes.' Petersen Sahib smiled. 'When thou hast seen the elephants dance. That is the proper time. Come to me when thou hast seen the elephants dance, and then I will let thee go into all the Keddahs.' *(The Keddahs were the stockades where the elephants were kept.)*

There was a roar of laughter, for that is an old joke among elephant-catchers, and it means just never. There are great cleared flat places hidden away in the forests that are called elephants' ball-rooms, but even these are only found by accident, and no man has ever seen the elephants dance. When a driver boasts of his skill and bravery the other drivers say, 'And when didst *thou* see the elephants dance?'

But that night, Kala Nag (his name meant 'Black Snake') broke loose, and went off into the jungle. Little Toomai went with him . . .

At last Kala Nag stood still between two tree-trunks at the very top of the hill. They were part of a circle of trees that grew round an irregular space of some three or four acres, and in all that space, as Little Toomai could see, the ground had been trampled down as hard as a brick floor. Some trees grew in the centre of the clearing, but their bark was rubbed away, and the white wood beneath showed all shiny and polished in the patches of moonlight. There were creepers hanging from the upper branches, and the bells of the flowers of the creepers, great waxy white things like convolvuluses, hung down fast asleep; but within the limits of the clearing there was not a single blade of green – nothing but the trampled earth.

The moonlight showed it all iron-grey, except where some elephants stood upon it, and their shadows were inky black. Little Toomai looked, holding his breath, with his eyes starting out of his head, and as he looked, more and more and more elephants swung out into the open from between the tree-trunks. Little Toomai could count only up to ten, and he counted again and again on his fingers till he lost count of the tens, and his head began to swim. Outside the clearing he could hear them crashing in the undergrowth as they worked their way up the hillside; but as soon as they were within the circle of the tree-trunks they moved like ghosts.

There were white-tusked wild males, with fallen leaves and nuts and twigs lying in the wrinkles of their necks and the folds of their ears; fat, slow-footed she-elephants, with restless little pinky-black calves only three or four feet high running under their stomachs; young elephants with their tusks just beginning to show, and very proud of them; lanky, scraggy old-maid elephants, with their hollow, anxious faces, and trunks like rough bark; savage old bull-elephants, scarred from shoulder to flank with great weals and cuts of bygone fights, and the caked dirt of their solitary mud-baths dropping from their shoulders; and there was one with a broken tusk and the marks of the full-stroke, the terrible drawing scrape, of a tiger's claws on his side.

They were standing head to head, or walking to and fro across the ground in couples, or rocking and swaying all by themselves — scores and scores of elephants.

Toomai knew that so long as he lay still on Kala Nag's neck nothing would happen to him; for even in the rush and scramble of a Keddah-drive a wild elephant does not reach up with his trunk and drag a man off the neck of a tame elephant; and these elephants were not thinking of men that night.

Once they started and put their ears forward when they heard the chinking of a leg-iron in the forest, but it was Pudmini, Petersen Sahib's pet elephant, her chain snapped off short, grunting, snuffling up the hillside. She must have broken her pickets, and come straight from Petersen Sahib's camp; and Little Toomai saw another elephant, one that he did not know, with deep rope-galls on his back and breast. He, too, must have run away from some camp in the hills about.

At last there was no sound of any more elephants moving in the forest, and Kala Nag rolled out from his station between the trees and into the middle of the crowd, clucking and gurgling, and all the elephants began to talk in their own tongue, and to move about.

Still lying down, Little Toomai looked down upon scores and scores of broad backs, and wagging ears, and tossing trunks, and little rolling eyes. He heard the click of tusks as they crossed other tusks by accident, and the dry rustle of trunks twined together, and the chafing of enormous sides and shoulders in the crowd, and the incessant flick and *hissh* of the great tails. Then a cloud came over the moon, and he sat in black darkness; but the quiet, steady hustling and the pushing and gurgling went on just the same.

He knew that there were elephants all round Kala Nag, and that there was no chance of backing him out of the assembly; so he set his teeth and shivered. In a Keddah at least there was torch-light and shouting, but here he was all alone in the dark, and once a trunk came up and touched him on the knee.

34

Then an elephant trumpeted, and they all took it up for five or ten terrible seconds. The dew from the trees above spattered down like rain on the unseen backs, and a dull booming noise began, not very loud at first, and Little Toomai could not tell what it was; but it grew and grew, and Kala Nag lifted up one fore-foot and then the other, and brought them down on the ground – one-two, one-two, as steadily as trip-hammers.

The elephants were stamping all together now, and it sounded like a war-drum beaten at the mouth of a cave. The dew fell from the trees till there was no more left to fall, and the booming went on, and the ground rocked and shivered, and Little Toomai put his hands up to his ears to shut out the sound. But it was all one gigantic jar that ran through him – this stamp of hundreds of heavy feet on the raw earth. One or twice he could feel Kala Nag and all the others surge forward a few strides, and the thumping would change to the crushing sound of juicy green things being bruised, but in a minute or two the boom of feet on hard earth began again.

A tree was creaking and groaning somewhere near him. He put out his arm and felt the bark, but Kala Nag moved forward, still tramping, and he could not tell where he was in the clearing. There was no sound from the elephants, except once, when two or three little calves squeaked together. Then he heard a thump and a shuffle, and the booming went on. It must have lasted fully two hours and Little Toomai ached in every nerve; but he knew by the smell of the night air that the dawn was coming.

The morning broke in one sheet of pale yellow behind the green hills, and the booming stopped with the first ray, as though the light had been an order. Before Little Toomai had got the ringing out of his head, before even he had shifted his position, there was not an elephant in sight except Kala Nag, Pudmini, and the elephant with the rope-galls, and there was neither sign nor whisper down the hillsides to show where the others had gone.

Little Toomai stared again and again. The clearing, as he remembered it, had grown in the night. Now he understood the trampling. The elephants had stamped out more room — had stamped the thick grass and juicy cane to trash, the trash into slivers, the slivers into tiny fibres, and the fibres into the hard earth.

WHY...

Why does an elephant wear red socks?

Because his others are being washed.

Two hours later, as Petersen Sahib was eating early breakfast, the elephants, who had been double-chained that night, began to trumpet, and Pudmini, mired to the shoulders, with Kala Nag, very footsore, shambled into the camp.

Little Toomai's face was grey and pinched, and his hair was full of leaves and drenched with dew; but he tried to salute Petersen Sahib, and cried faintly, 'The dance — the elephant-dance! I have seen it!' As Kala Nag sat down, he slid off his neck in a dead faint.

Petersen Sahib went to look at the dance-place, and found it was just as Little Toomai had said. So from that day forward, Little Toomai was known as Toomai of the Elephants, because he had seen what no man had seen before — the dance of the elephants.

Elephants through the ages

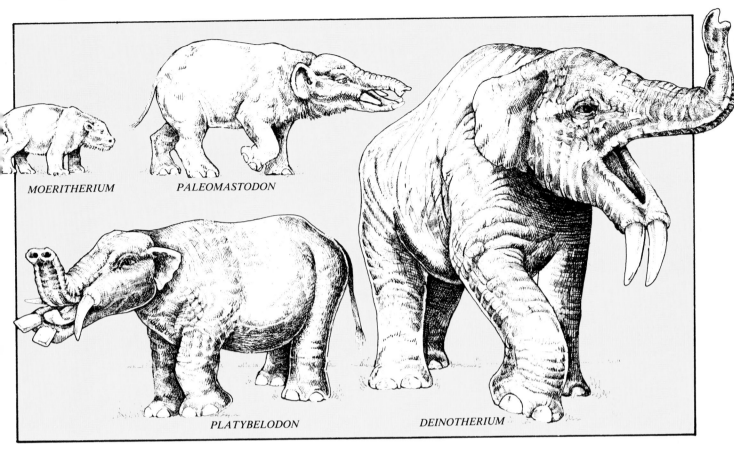

MOERITHERIUM   PALEOMASTODON

PLATYBELODON   DEINOTHERIUM

There have been elephants on Earth for over fifty million years, and during that time there have been more than three hundred different kinds. The very first elephant we know about was only sixty centimetres tall, and was called Moeritherium *(Mo-er-rith-ee-ree-um)*.

The early elephants didn't look much like the elephants of today. Some of them ate roots, for example, so they had jaws shaped like shovels.

Over millions and millions of years, elephants became larger and larger, and they began to have trunks. Two of their front teeth grew longer and longer and became tusks. Then the Mammoth appeared, and this was even bigger than the elephants we see nowadays. During the long years when the Earth was covered in ice and snow (the Ice Ages), Mammoths were covered in thick hair to keep them warm. We know what Mammoths looked like because early men hunted it for food, and painted pictures of it on his cave walls. There is also in Russia a baby Mammoth which was preserved in the Arctic ice for thousands of years.

In the modern world, there are only two kinds of African elephant left, and only four

Mammoth

kinds of Asian elephant. And of the Asian elephants, three are in danger of becoming *extinct* (that is, there will soon be none left at all), the Sumatran, the Sri Lankan and the Malaysian (which is very hairy).

Can elephants be trained?

Because their trunks are so strong that they can carry heavy logs of wood, elephants are used in the teak forests in India and Burma. They can be trained to understand as many as thirty different commands, such as 'turn to the right', or 'lift the chain'. All the training of an elephant is done by one man – in India he is called a *mahout,* and in Burma, an *oozie*. Elephants and their handlers learn to trust one another, and they become great friends.

What is the difference between African and Asian elephants?

Asian elephants are smaller than African elephants, and they have much smaller ears, with the upper edge curled forwards.

38

How long does an elephant take to produce a baby elephant?

If it's a boy *(bull)* calf, it takes twenty-two months. A girl *(cow)* calf takes only twenty months. This is much longer than humans, who take nine months to produce a baby — and it's the same for boy or girl. A new-born baby elephant however weighs about ninety kilograms (200 lbs) — something like thirty times as heavy as a new-born human baby!

When is an elephant fully grown?

An elephant is not fully grown until it is twenty-five years old. For the first four or five years, it is given milk by its mother. Other elephants in the herd help by collecting and cutting food into small pieces for the baby. All the young elephants in the herd are kept together in a 'play group', and one of the adults acts as a babysitter. This is so that the mothers have time to feed themselves.

This photograph shows the two upper cheek teeth with their grinding surfaces. Each tooth is as big as a house brick.

How do you tell an elephant's age?

By its teeth. In order to chew all the food it needs, the elephant has very big cheek teeth or molars which have large ridged grinding surfaces to crush the food. The elephant has six sets of these teeth during its life. The first are about the size of matchboxes, and the final set are as big as the bricks in a house. The final set does not appear until the elephant is about thirty-three years old.

Do elephants live a long time?

They live up to sixty-five years old in captivity, but not quite so long in the wild.

The Elephant's Petals

by Brian Patten
illustrated by Graham Round

'There was once a flower that could walk, and there was once an elephant no larger than a flower. They became friends, and stayed together on a hill . . .'

The elephant was sitting on the hill, looking at the clouds which all looked like very large elephants. Some days they looked like boats, and other days they looked like bushes, but today they looked best. He was very happy looking up until he noticed that the flower was acting rather peculiar.

It kept on walking round him, stopping every now and then and nodding its head, as if it were agreeing with itself about something.

'What's wrong?' asked the elephant.

'It has just occurred to me,' said the flower, 'that you are a freak.'

'A freak!' cried the elephant. 'A *freak*!'

'Yes, a freak,' repeated the flower. 'You haven't got any petals. In fact you don't even possess an ordinary little leaf.'

The elephant had a small think.

'No, you're the freak,' he said. 'You haven't got a trunk.'

'Nonsense,' said the flower. 'I've seen plenty of things with petals and leaves – like blossoms and creepers and trees and bushes. Why, even the birds sometimes carry leaves – but they don't carry trunks. I've never seen anything with a trunk.'

'What about the trees, then?' said the elephant. 'What about them? They have trunks.'

'No, they don't,' said the flower. 'They have a very long and very thick stalk, like mine but a lot bigger. Anyway, it's not the same thing.'

'Yes, it is.'

'No, it isn't.'

'Yes, it is. They have leaves and trunks.'

'It isn't the same,' said the flower, getting angry.

'Of course it is,' said the elephant. 'You're just a small tree. More a small tree than I am a small elephant.'

'I'm not,' roared the flower. 'Trees have long wooden stems and you have a small, funny trunk. You're a freak! Try and name me something that has a trunk like yours.'

The elephant tried, but he couldn't. 'Then everything is a freak except me,' he shouted, and he ran down the hill as fast as he could. When he reached the bottom of the hill and was hidden in the jungle, he could still hear the flower shouting at the top of its voice, 'You're a freak! You've got no petals!'

And that was their first argument. The elephant grew very worried. Not about the argument but about the fact that he had no petals. 'Perhaps I should have some,' he thought. The flower had been very convincing.

Every time the elephant heard one of the jungle creatures coming towards him he scurried away behind a small bush or a large stone and kept very still. He was quite embarrassed about having no petals.

Then the elephant had an idea.

Farther upstream there was a native village.

'I'll go and see the witch-doctor,' thought the elephant.

But even the witch-doctor had no spells for growing petals on elephants, even very tiny ones.

'Oh well,' thought the elephant, 'I'll just have to go and find some old leaves myself and stick them on me.' And so he did.

The elephant walked round the jungle collecting fallen leaves and petals of all kinds. He made a huge pile of them, much bigger than himself. Then the elephant went and stood under a gum tree until he was covered over in the messy stuff. Running back to the pile of petals and leaves he jumped into the middle of them, rolling over and over. They all stuck to the elephant.

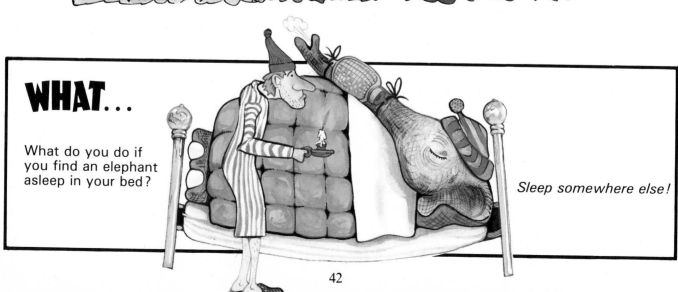

WHAT...

What do you do if you find an elephant asleep in your bed?

Sleep somewhere else!

42

All this time the flower had been sitting on the hill wondering what the elephant was doing.

'Maybe he's run away for ever,' thought the flower. And that made the flower very miserable. It decided to go and look for the elephant and apologise. After all, it was a silly argument. 'Elephants are elephants and flowers are flowers,' it decided to say when it found the elephant. It wandered down the hill and into the jungle, but it could not find the elephant.

At the edge of a path down which the flower was walking there was a strange little bump, entirely covered in petals and leaves.

'Funny,' thought the flower. 'I've never noticed that before.' It decided to sit on the bump and wait there just in case the elephant came past. But, before the flower could sit down, the bump gave a little groan and hurried away.

'That's a strange bump,' thought the flower. 'It's got little fat legs like an elephant. I'd better follow it.'

As the flower walked behind the bump, which did not seem able to see where it was going, it heard it say, 'I'm fed up. I'm very fed up indeed.' Then crash! – the bump banged into a very large tree. It staggered about in circles, groaning all the time. The flower was deciding whether or not to ask the bump where it wanted to go and take it there, when they suddenly came to a shallow pond. Before the flower could shout a warning, the bump, still dizzy, staggered in. Splash! went the pond. Groan! went the bump.

When the flower reached the pond it was full of petals and leaves, but there was no bump to be seen anywhere. In its place was the elephant, up to its neck in water.

'How peculiar,' thought the flower.

'I'm learning how to swim,' lied the elephant.

'That's good,' said the flower. 'I thought you might be drowning yourself because I said you're a freak.'

'Certainly not,' said the elephant. 'I don't like petals on me one bit.'

'That's good,' said the flower. And then it apologised and made a little speech it had prepared, about how elephants didn't need petals after all, and how flowers didn't need trunks either.

The elephant thought it was a marvellous speech and it got up out of the water and went home to look at the clouds again.

43

Pope Leo's Elephant

by John Lawrence
illustrated by Martin Aitchison

The Vatican City is a special city in the heart of Rome. It is the home of the Pope, and many long years ago it was also the home of Paolo, son of a chair-bearer in the service of Pope Leo X. Pope Leo was a wise Pope and Paolo's father was happy to serve him.

One day Paolo watched a ceremony from a balcony in the Pope's palace. An ambassador had come from the King of Portugal to offer the Pope a splendid gift – an elephant from the distant land of India! The Pope accepted gladly, for it was well known that he loved all birds and animals.

Paolo's eyes shone as he listened. An elephant! What sort of beast was an elephant? Paolo's mind was filled with strange and wonderful images as he watched the servants of the Pope make ready for the arrival of the animal.

Everybody was excited. The carpenters sang as they prepared a stall for the elephant and the farmers called to each other as they brought in food and hay from the countryside.

The Pope himself came to watch the preparations, carried aloft in his chair. Paolo's father told the Pope that his son had a favour to ask.

Trembling a little, Paolo knelt before the Pope and begged to be allowed to help with the elephant. The Pope smiled and nodded. Paolo's heart was full.

Soon it was the day of the elephant's arrival. A procession was held and there was rejoicing in the streets of Rome, for few of the citizens had seen so mighty a beast before. 'Leofante! Leofante!' they shouted, and from that moment Pope Leo's elephant had a name.

Leofante was tired when he reached the Vatican. He saw Paolo and a group of attendants standing nearby and trumpeted noisily, swinging his trunk from side to side. Paolo stared at Leofante in wonder but was not afraid. Stepping forward he caught hold of the elephant's Papal trappings and led the huge beast to his new home, speaking softly to him all the while. It was the beginning of a friendship, for Paolo and Leofante soon became inseparable.

44

Leofante was gentle and docile and the people of Rome grew to love him. But Paolo loved him best of all.

Pope Leo often came to see Leofante. He was proud of his elephant, and he asked the great artist Raphael to paint a picture of the animal. Paolo set to work scrubbing and cleaning Leofante to make him fit for the eyes of the Master.

Raphael was enchanted with Leofante. He made many sketches and drawings of the elephant. Paolo thought the pictures were magnificent, especially the one which showed Leofante being raised up to Heaven by myriads of angels.

But life was not all leisure for Paolo and Leofante. Raphael the artist was also an architect, and it was his job to supervise the building of the vast new cathedral, St Peter's. He realised that a strong animal could help the workmen to move heavy loads. The carpenters built a ramp for Leofante so that he could carry timber and stone to the builders.

Paolo and Leofante were busy all day long. Sometimes a platform was raised on to Leofante's back so that Raphael could sit in comfort and watch the work going on about him as the great cathedral began to take shape.

WHY...
Why do elephants swim upside down?

So they don't tread on the fish.

One day, while the builders were having their lunch in the square, Paolo and Leofante took a last load to the top of the ramp. As they turned to go Leofante stopped, waving his trunk in the air. He seemed to be sniffing. Paolo, too, stopped short and sniffed the air. He could smell burning! 'Fire! Fire!' he shouted, as smoke suddenly billowed from a huge pile of wood shavings nearby and flames licked at the walls.

'Hurry, Leofante!' said Paolo. He scrambled on to the elephant's back and together they rushed down the ramp.

While Paolo shouted for help, Leofante lumbered to a fountain and took a deep draught of water into his trunk. Back up the ramp he hurried until he reached the fire. With a mighty snort he sent a stream of water on to the flames. Up and down the ramp he went, filling his trunk with water each time. Paolo urged him on, and they were joined by the carpenters and masons, who came puffing up the ramp with buckets of water.

Soon the fire was under control but news of it had spread, and a crowd had gathered outside. Paolo heard their cry: 'The Pope is coming! The Pope is coming!'

Pope Leo appeared, carried by his bearers, who brought him to the scene of the fire. At that very moment there was a terrible rumbling in the roof above the Pope's head. One of the beams, weakened by the fire, was giving way!

Quick as a flash Paolo and Leofante moved forward. They were just in time! The roof beam crumbled, and sagged on to the elephant's broad back as the chair-bearers hurried Pope Leo away to safety.

And there Leofante stayed, patiently and calmly, as the workmen put up supports to hold the roof in place. Then Paolo and Leofante walked away as the crowd cheered. 'Leofante! Leofante! Viva Leofante!' they shouted.

Leofante was a hero! He had saved the Pope. And he had put out the fire.

The Pope ordered a marble fountain to be made in honour of his brave and gentle elephant, and Paolo and Leofante lived happily in the Vatican for the rest of their days.

The Animal Fair

I went to the animal fair
All the birds and the beasts were there,
The gay baboon by the light of the moon
Was combing his yellow hair.
The monkey fell from his bunk
And dropped on the elephant's trunk.
The elephant sneezed, and went down on his knees
And what became of the mon-key, mon-key,
mon-key, mon-key, monk?

How do elephants 'talk' to each other?

To start with, they use their trunks to touch each other; in this way they can recognise their friends. When companions meet, they make soft 'peeping' and 'rumbling' noises — they can also recognise each other by the sound of their voices, because elephants have very good hearing.

When an elephant flaps its ears against the side of its head, this means that there is danger. All the members of the herd will then gather close together for safety. Mother elephants also call their young to them in this way.

Herds of elephants have scouts who go ahead to make sure that there is no danger. The scouts will trumpet a special 'all clear' signal when they know it is safe.

48

The Ant and the Elephant

by Bill Peet
illustrated by James Hodgson

One morning a tiny ant crawled up a tall blade of jungle grass for a view of the river. All at once he was caught by a breeze that sent him sailing off into the swirling water. Just when it seemed he would be swept downstream and gone for ever, the ant grabbed on to a branch caught in the current and scrambled to safety.

There the ant remained stranded wondering what he would do, when he spied a mud turtle creeping along the riverbank.

'Oh, Mr Hardshell!' called the ant in his wee, small voice. 'Would you be so kind as to give me a lift back to dry land? It's a nice day for a swim.'

The old turtle turned his head slowly. After a long look at the ant, he said, 'I've had my swim for today, and besides, if I went racing about helping everyone who was in trouble I'd have no time left to relax.' Then the turtle tottered on his way to find a place where he could sun himself.

When the turtle came to a flat, warm rock, he crept slowly up the edge. Suddenly he went toppling backward and landed upside down.

'Blast it all,' he muttered. 'Dad blame it!' And he began thrashing out with his legs, desperately trying to right himself. But all the kicking could do was to send him rocking about on his shell. That was all.

As he stretched his stringy neck looking about for help, the turtle spied a hornbill roosting on her nest high on a tree limb.

'Oh, Mrs Bigbill!' he called. 'Would you mind helping me back to my feet? With one flip of your beak I'm sure you could do it.'

'I could,' snapped the bird, 'but I won't. This will teach you not to be so clumsy.'

49

As she leaned down to say more, the hornbill tipped the nest and her one big egg rolled out to go tumbling all the way to the ground. Luckily it landed in a clump of fluff-twuff weeds without so much as a crack.

'Thank goodness,' she cried, when she found the egg all in one piece. Then, seizing it in her beak, she fluttered her wings as she tried to take off. But her oversized beak plus the cumbersome egg were too much of a load. Still she kept on furiously thrashing the air until her wings were worn to a frazzle.

As the miserable bird sat there staring helplessly at the egg, a giraffe came striding along.

'Oh, Mr Greatneck!' she called. 'You've come just at the right time. If I perched on your head with the egg in my beak, you could carry us back up to my nest.'

'Indeed no!' scoffed the proud giraffe. 'If I did such a thing how silly I would look. I'll have no one laughing at me. No, indeed!' And Mr Greatneck went on his way with his head held high, nibbling at the treetops.

He was so intent upon the tasty leaves he didn't notice the tangle-dangle vine until it was twisted up around one leg.

50

became. Finally, his legs were so tightly tied up in the vine he couldn't budge.

As he stood there in the tangle, he spied a lion heading his way.

'What good luck,' thought the giraffe. 'With those great claws of his he could rip this vine to shreds in one swipe.'

'Oh, Mr Bigpaw!' he called to the lion. 'Just look at me!'

The lion took one look, then burst into a great roaring laugh. 'Ho! Ho! That is funny. Ho! Ho! I see what you mean. Ho! Ho! Ho!' And, laughing merrily, he went on his way through the jungle.

The lion was still laughing to himself as he flopped down in a patch of shade for a bit of a catnap. He flopped down with such a *whump!* it upset a huge boulder which was all set to topple. To the lion's surprise it rolled over and came down right upon his tail.

With a furious roar he leaped to his feet, tugging frantically to free himself. But he soon found it was useless to struggle. He could never get loose unless he was willing to part with his tail.

'Here now!' snorted the giraffe with an angry kick. 'How dare you!' The kick merely gave the vine an extra twist which tightened its grip. Then in a fury the giraffe began kicking wildly about with all four legs. The more he kicked the more entangled he

As he sat there growling over his bad luck, a rhino came along.

'Oh, Mr Hornyhead!' he called. 'Would you mind bumping this stupid boulder off my tail? One nudge of your great snout would do it.'

'I would,' said the rhino, 'if you could think of some way to return the favour.'

'Right now,' sighed the lion, 'all I can think of is my poor tail.'

'Too bad,' said the rhino, and he went lumbering off through the trees.

The rhino never bothered to watch where he was going. With his great horn out front he went ploughing straight ahead through the brambles and brush, when all of a sudden *zump!* − he blundered head-on into a stump with his great horn stuck deep into it.

'Out of my way, you stupid stump!' He snorted. And with a furious lunge he tried to knock over the stump. This drove the horn still deeper. Then with a mighty tug he tried pulling himself free, but the stump refused to let go. At last the rhino realised he was hopelessly stuck.

So the rhino, the lion, the giraffe, the hornbill, the turtle, and the ant were left in deep trouble. That would have been that if a jolly big somebody hadn't decided to take a stroll through the jungle that day.

It was a huge elephant with such great spreading ears he could hear the slightest sound − the faint rustle of a leaf, the least snap of a twig, or even the tiny voice of an ant calling.

He reached his long trunk out over the river, inviting the ant to climb aboard, then carried him safely back to dry land.

'How can I ever thank you enough!' cried the grateful ant.

'It was no big thing,' said the elephant.

'But it was a big thing for me,' said the ant. 'It was everything!' And he scurried away through the grass.

'If you've got time to bother with a nothing of an ant,' grumbled the old turtle, 'how about me?'

'You *are* in a pickle,' said the elephant, and with the tip of his trunk he flipped the turtle back on to his feet.

Then without a word of thanks the old codger went tottering away down the bank to disappear in the river.

'If you can help an ugly old turtle,' squawked the hornbill, 'the least you can do is put my lovely egg back in the nest.'

'The very least I can do,' agreed the elephant, and holding the egg gently in his trunk, he carried it up to the nest.

'It's a wonder you didn't crack it,' snapped the bird, as she settled down on to the egg.

'Say now,' chuckled the elephant, when he came upon the giraffe, 'that's what I call a funny fix.'

'Not funny to me!' snorted the giraffe. 'Not one bit funny!'

'Then I'll try not to laugh,' said the big fellow, searching through the vine with his trunk to get at the worst of the tangle.

It took a few minutes to undo the dozens of knots that gripped the long legs. Once they were loose, the vine fell limply to the ground.

'Well, I must say, it's about time,' snorted the snooty giraffe, as he went gallopity-clopping away.

'What have we here?' asked the elephant, when he came to the lion.

'We have a big, stupid, bumbling boulder!' growled the lion. 'That's what!'

'Then be off, stupid boulder!' And the huge tusker heaved the boulder into the air with his trunk and sent it tumbling.

Once he was free, the lion gave his tail a few switches to make sure it was working. 'What a relief,' sighed the lion. 'Some day when I'm in a better mood I must remember to thank you.'

WHAT...

What is grey, has four legs, and a trunk?

A mouse going on holiday.

53

'No hurry,' said the elephant.

He continued on his way through the jungle, where he soon found the hopelessly stuck rhino.

'I can pull you free,' said the elephant, 'if your tail can stand one mighty tug.'

'Right now it's my snout I'm worried about,' groaned the rhino, 'so jerk away!'

Gripping the rhino's tail tightly in his trunk, the elephant reared back, and with one almighty jerk the rhino went sailing free of the stump to land with one big *blump!*

'That was one whale of a jerk,' muttered the rhino. 'I hope you got some fun out of it.'

'It was a pleasure,' smiled the elephant, as he went merrily on his way.

He was enormously pleased with himself after all the good deeds he had done that day.

'Everyone has his troubles,' he chuckled. 'Everyone but big me. I'll never get into a fix where I need help. That's one thing for sure.' The elephant didn't suspect there was a deep ravine just ahead. It was too well hidden by scatter-flat ferns.

Before he knew it, he had tumbled straight into it, landing with a seven-ton *thud* that shook the whole jungle. He was wedged so deep and in such a position that his trunk and his legs were useless.

'It serves me right,' he muttered, 'for feeling so almighty big and all-powerful. Now I'm the one who needs help.'

'Help!' he bellowed. 'Help! Help! Help!' Then he waited anxiously for a reply. He waited for hours, staring up at the sky until it faded into evening and a deep stillness settled over the jungle.

It was so quiet his great spreading ears caught the sound of footsteps — tiny, tiny footsteps from somewhere above.

'Who's there?' asked the elephant.

'It's me,' said a wee, small voice. 'The ant you rescued this morning and all my ant friends. Ninety-five thousand of them.'

'I know ants are amazingly strong,' said the elephant, 'but surely you don't expect to lift me out of here.'

'We can try,' said the ant. 'Come on, my friends, let's get to work.'

Suddenly down the steep wall of the ravine came a teeming horde of ants swarming under the elephant. Then all together they began chanting, 'Heave ho! Heave ho! Up you go! Up you go!' And to the elephant's amazement he felt himself moving upward. Slowly but surely, just an inch at a time, the tireless ants hoisted their huge burden up the wall.

'Heave ho! Up you go! Don't lose your grip! Don't anyone trip!' And at last, under a bright full moon they set the elephant down in the scatter-flat ferns.

'That was tremendous!' cried the elephant. 'I can't believe it!'

'It was nothing,' replied the ninety-five thousand ants.

'Nothing for you,' said the elephant, 'but a mighty big thing for me. Now if you'll climb aboard I'll give you a ride back to your ant hill.'

'I'm not a bit tired,' said one ant, 'but I would like a ride. I've never ridden on an elephant.'

'Neither have I,' cried all the others, and they swarmed up the elephant's legs on to his back. Then away they went herumpity-bumpity clumpity-hump — the mighty big and the mighty small, off through the jungle together.

The Grasshopper and the Elephant

Way down south where bananas grow,
A grasshopper stepped on an elephant's toe.
The elephant said, with tears in his eyes,
'Pick on somebody your own size.'

Is anyone helping the elephants?

The World Wildlife Fund is trying to organise protection for the Asian varieties, because some of them could disappear in the next few years. There are now some National Parks in South Asian countries where the forests will be preserved. There are also big National Parks in Africa where elephants and their environment can be protected. Wardens patrol these parks to keep poachers away. Asian elephants are in danger because large areas of the forests where they live are being cut down each year to provide farming land. African elephants are in danger because of poachers who are after ivory.

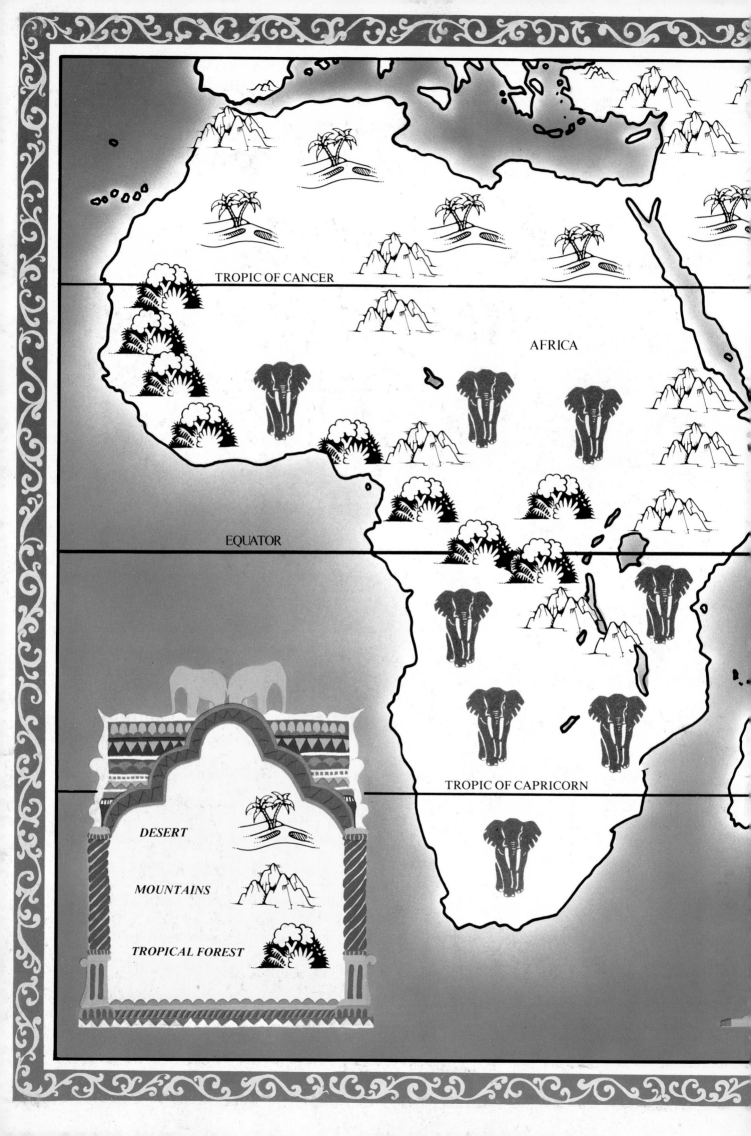

TROPIC OF CANCER

AFRICA

EQUATOR

TROPIC OF CAPRICORN

DESERT

MOUNTAINS

TROPICAL FOREST